This Little Tiger book belongs to:

_____

_____

_____

_____

To Bridie
A.M.

To Alice, with love
G.W.

LITTLE TIGER PRESS
An imprint of Magi Publications
1 The Coda Centre, 189 Munster Road,
London SW6 6AW, UK
www.littletigerpress.com
First published in Great Britain 1998
by Little Tiger Press, London
This edition published 2008
Text copyright © Alan MacDonald 1998
Illustrations copyright © Gwyneth Williamson 1998
Alan MacDonald and Gwyneth Williamson have
asserted their rights to be identified as the author
and illustrator of this work under the Copyright,
Designs and Patents Act, 1988
ISBN 978-1-84506-504-1
Printed in China
1 2 3 4 5 6 7 8 9 10

BEWARE of the BEARS!

by Alan MacDonald

illustrated by Gwyneth Williamson

LITTLE TIGER PRESS

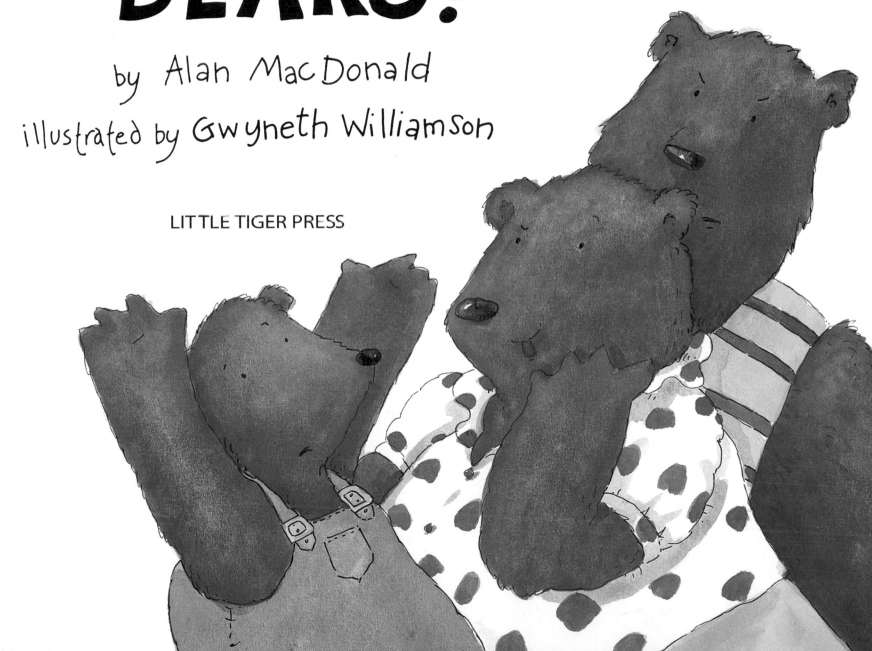

When the three bears saw what Goldilocks had done to their little cottage, they were hopping mad.

Their porridge eaten!

Chairs broken!

Beds bounced on!

"Go after her! Find out where she lives!" ordered Daddy Bear.

Baby Bear jumped on
his scooter and sped
after Goldilocks.

In no time at all he was back.
"She lives on the far side of the forest,"
panted Baby Bear. "And what's more,
she's just gone out again and left
her door unlocked."

"Good!" said Mommy Bear.
"What are we waiting for?
Let's see how *she* likes having
uninvited guests."

Baby Bear led the way through the
forest to Goldilocks's cottage. The door
was unlocked, just as he'd said.

On the breakfast table were several open boxes.
"This isn't porridge," sniffed Mommy Bear.

Baby Bear read the labels. "Wheetos, Munch Flakes,
and Puffo Pops."

"Sounds all right to me," said Daddy Bear. "Pour away,
Baby-o!"

"These Wheetos are too sweet," said Daddy Bear.
"These Munch Flakes are too noisy," said Mommy Bear.
"But these Puffo Pops are just right," said Baby Bear, aiming a spoonful toward Daddy Bear.

The Puffo Pops hit Daddy Bear in the eye. He launched
a spoonful of Wheetos. They splattered all over
Mommy Bear's best blouse.

Soon cereal was flying left and right, until the floors,
the walls, and the ceiling were dripping with brown goo.

Then Baby Bear turned on the radio.
"Let's dance!" he squealed.

Mommy and Daddy
Bear tangoed on
the table.
"This table's
too slippy," said
Daddy Bear.

They did the cha-cha
around the curtains.
"These curtains are
too rippy," said
Mommy Bear.

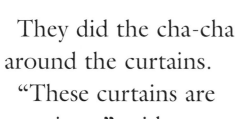

"But this sofa's just right,"
squeaked Baby Bear, so they
all jumped on the sofa and
did the bossa nova
until . . .

they went right through it!

Next the three bears looked upstairs.
There were lots of things to try
in the bathroom.
"The shaving cream's too creamy,"
grumbled Daddy Bear.

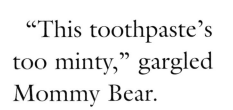

"This toothpaste's
too minty," gargled
Mommy Bear.

"But this bubble bath is
just right," cried Baby
Bear from beneath a
mountain of suds.
"All right, here we come,"
said Mommy Bear.

They had a wonderful time splashing in the bath.

Once they were clean and the bathroom a mess,
they moved on to the bedroom.
"These pajamas are too tight," said Daddy Bear,
bursting the buttons.
"This mattress is too
lumpy," said Mommy
Bear, bouncing up
and down.
"But these pillows are
just right," said Baby
Bear. "Just right for
a pillow fight."

Baby Bear biffed Mommy Bear. Mommy Bear whacked Daddy Bear. Pillows split open, filling the air with clouds of feathers. Suddenly Daddy Bear stopped.
"Listen!" he said. "I hear someone."
Quietly, the three bears crept downstairs.

Goldilocks was in the kitchen. Daddy Bear, Mommy Bear, and Baby Bear gleefully spied on her from behind the door.

Goldilocks gasped when she saw the cereal splattered all over the walls.

Her eyes grew large when she saw the ripped curtains and the gigantic hole in the sofa.

She whistled when she saw the flooded bathroom decorated with shaving foam and toothpaste.

Next Goldilocks went into the bedroom.
She stared openmouthed at the broken
bed covered with feathers.

Then the three bears jumped out from
behind the door.

"Surprise!" they shouted.
"We thought *we'd* pay *you* a visit,"
said Mommy Bear.
Goldilocks looked at them,
then back at the room . . .

and to the bears' astonishment, she threw back her head and laughed until her hair shook like golden springs.

"What's so funny," asked Mommy Bear.

"But aren't you mad at what we've done?" added Daddy Bear.

"This isn't my house," giggled Goldilocks.

"But it must be," said Baby Bear, "I saw you go in."

"Oh, that," said Goldilocks. "The door was open, so I thought I'd look around. I'm always sneaking into other people's houses. I only came back because I left my teddy bear behind."

"Then if it's not your house, *whose house is it?*" asked Daddy Bear. "Oh help!" squeaked Baby Bear, looking out of the window . . .

fantastic reads from Little Tiger Press

BEWARE of the BEARS!
Alan MacDonald
Gwyneth Williamson

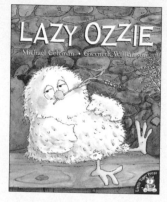

LAZY OZZIE
Michael Coleman • Gwyneth Williamson

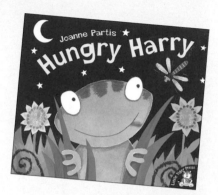

Joanne Partis
Hungry Harry

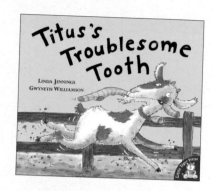

Titus's Troublesome Tooth
LINDA JENNINGS
Gwyneth Williamson

Little Tiger's big surprise!
Julie Sykes • Tim Warnes

Have you got my Purr?
Judy West
Tim Warnes

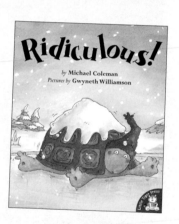

Ridiculous!
by Michael Coleman
Pictures by Gwyneth Williamson

Martin Hall and Catherine Walters
Charlie and Tess

for information regarding any of the above titles
or for our catalogue, please contact us:
Little Tiger Press, 1 The Coda Centre,
189 Munster Road, London SW6 6AW, UK
Tel: +44 (0)20 7385 6333 fax: +44 (0)20 7385 7333
E-mail: info@littletiger.co.uk
www.littletigerpress.com

IT COULD HAVE BEEN WORSE
A.H. Benjamin • Tim Warnes

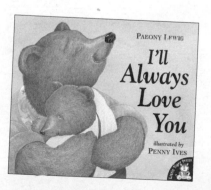

PAEONY LEWIS
I'll Always Love You
illustrated by
PENNY IVES